ATHENA MAE
SAVES
THE PLANET
I0827737
Written by Nicolette Jahnke
Illustrated by Owen Eaton

ISBN#

978-1-7349171-0-9

DEDICATED
TO THE WORLD

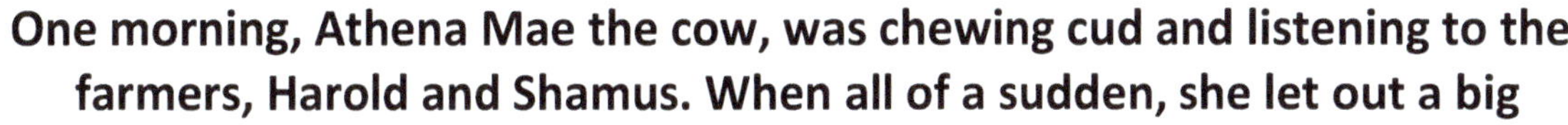

One morning, Athena Mae the cow, was chewing cud and listening to the farmers, Harold and Shamus. When all of a sudden, she let out a big

FART !

It was so loud, everyone jumped.

"PEE YEW!" said Shamus.

"KELP TO THE RESCUE," said Harold.

"If the smell doesn't get us, the methane will."

"KELP?

THAT SEAWEED STUFF? " asked Shamus.

““Yep!” said Harold.
“Some scientist found that feeding your cows kelp,
takes out the methane in their burps and farts, but not the smell.”

“Wow, that’s amazing! Where do you get it?” asked Shamus.

“I don’t know?” shrugged Harold.

Just then the milking bell rang, along with another loud

FART.

“Oh no, there goes the planet!” yelled Shamus.

“DA TA DA DA!

KELP TO THE RESCUE.”

“

?
Kelp?

DING, DING, DING!

Slowly, Athena made her way to the barn, but couldn't help but wonder, methane, kelp, what were those things? Why was she like a ticking time bomb?

As she waited in line for her turn at the milking machine, she asked the other mothers what they knew about methane and kelp. Did they know they were destroying the planet?

Not a mother knew a thing.

What were they going to do?

Someone needed to find this, kelp, to get rid of the methane.

Someone needed to save the planet.

COULD ATHENA DO IT, COULD SHE BECOME.........

SUPERCOW?
KELP

COULD SHE SAVE THE PLANET? SHE HAD TO, BUT HOW?

Herbie, the farms pug, he'd know. Herbie loved to eat.

"Herbie, wake up, wake up! Do you know what kelp is and where I can find it? It's really, really important!"

said Herbie.

"It's those froufrou leaves humans eat! Oh, wait a minute, oops, that's kale.

KELP? KELP? KELP?

Hmmm, let me yelp around. Come back, in about a half an hour."

"Oh thank-you Herbie," Athena said, as she dashed off.

Spotting her calves playing in the pasture, she let out a **BIG MOO.**

All three scampered up and asked,

"WHAT IS IT MOO-MMY."

"I have to go save the planet. There's no time for questions. So please be good and don't fight. Just remember, I love you very, very much. I've got to go, there's no time to waste."

She kissed each of them and with tears in her eyes, turned and headed back to the barn.

"Well, Herbie, did you find out about the kelp," she asked.

"In the barn there's a swallow named Bray, he knows!"

"Oh, thank-you Herbie, thank-you, do you know,

YOU MAY JUST HAVE

SAVED THE PLANET!"

Hurrying inside she yelled, “Hello! Bray, hello! Hello, Bray!”
Suddenly, a swallow swooped down.

“Hi, I’m Bray! Herbie says you’re looking for kelp. My cousin Glenn, a seagull, brought some from the ocean. Go to the ocean and you’ll find your kelp!”

“THE OCEAN?” asked Athena.

“What’s an ocean and where would I find this, ocean?”

“I don’t know,” replied Bray.” I’ve never been to the ocean. Glenn says it’s a lot of water. Maybe ask by the stream if they know. Sorry! That’s the best I can do.”

“Oh, thank-you Bray, thank-you, you don’t know how much you’ve done,

YOU MAY JUST HAVE

SAVED THE PLANET!”

The stream Bray was talking about was outside of the pasture. After Athena told Tammy the gray squirrel about the methane and kelp, Tammy jumped on Athena's back and opened the padlock for her.

"Thank-you Tammy, thank-you, I think

YOU MAY JUST HAVE SAVED THE PLANET!"

Up and down Athena wandered, up and down, yelling, "Anyone know what an ocean is? Where an ocean is?"

Suddenly, she was splashed in the face.

"Over here," said a salmon. "My name's Shirley. You're looking for the ocean? I just came from there, what a trip. I'm going to miss it. It's so beautiful, so much food, so many colors, so much room to move in. I never would have left, but we salmon need to go back to where we were born, to spawn. It's our circle of life. You'll love it there!"

"Oh, I'm not going to live by the ocean," said Athena.
"I just need to bring back kelp for my children!
Do you know what kelp is?"

"Kelp, yeah, the ocean's full of kelp! Your pasture's full of grass!
Well, the ocean's full of kelp!"

"Oh, Shirley, you don't know how happy you've made me.
You see I just learned I have a problem, when I burp and expel gas,
I emit methane and methane is BAD for the planet,
but they've discovered that kelp takes away the methane
in my burps and gas. So, if I don't get that kelp,
I may not see my children grow up and have children.
Your children may not make the salmon circle of life.
The planet could be doomed all because of me!
That's why I need to bring back kelp for the rest of the farm
and farms down the road; I need to bring kelp to all the cows
and calves in the world. I'm just one little cow,
but I'm going to try!"

As she spoke, she felt stronger and stronger. **MAYBE, JUST MAYBE SHE COULD BECOME…..**

SUPERCOW!

"Well this is just one little stream and it turns into one big river
and it flows into a gigantic ocean," said Shirley.
"So, one little cow can make a difference.
Just follow this stream and you'll get your kelp.
But, how are you going to bring it back to the rest of the cows?"

"I hadn't thought about that."

"I'm sure you'll work it out. I'm sorry but I've got to go,
my future babies need me to get home to spawn,"
said Shirley. "So we'll ALL be counting on you."

"Thank-you Shirley, thank-you, I'm pretty sure

YOU MAY JUST HAVE

SAVED THE PLANET!"

Two birds suddenly swooped down and landed on Athena's back.
It was Bray and his dad, Kyler, they came to help.

"Oh Bray, I know how to get to the ocean.
Now I just have to figure out how to bring the kelp
back to the rest of the cows."

In the meantime, Tammy had been trying to figure out
how to contain Athena and the rest of the cows' burps and gas
until they got the kelp.

There was a lot of figuring out going on.

Mel the mole! He'd know what to do! Humans buried their gas in pipes,
so Mel could bury the cow's gas in tunnels.

Tammy looked for a mound of dirt and started to dig,
calling down into the hole, "Mel, Mel, are you in there? We need you, Mel!"

Bray and his dad flew up and down the stream calling for Mel,
while Athena tried not to fart or burp!

Way downstream up popped Mel and his wife Laurie.

"Hey, can't you be a little quieter? It's the kids nap time,
what's so urgent?" they asked.

When they got to Mel and Laurie, a large group of animals had gathered.
Tammy told all of them of Athena's problem.
She asked if there was any way Mel could tunnel Athena's
and the rest of the cows' gas and burps, to a safe place.

Mel looked down at his sleeping children, over to his wife and said,
"That's a real dilemma we've got. Let me think about it."

So, he thought, and he thought, and he thought.
They all grew very impatient!

TIME WAS RUNNING OUT

TO SAVE THE PLANET!

They needed to get to the kelp.

DING, DING, DING!

A little bell went off. Mel had a plan!

"There's an old garbage dump with all kinds of plastic pipe and tubes," said Mel.

He took a stick and began to draw his contraption in the dirt.

"We'll outfit all the cows with these and then we'll tunnel the gas to the silo. I'm going to need to get a squirrel and rabbit brigade, to help the mole brigade attach them to the cows."

"Oh, thank-you Mel, thank-you, guess what,

YOU MAY JUST HAVE SAVED THE PLANET!"

said Athena.

"I better get going. Bray, can you and your dad fly ahead and ask the other animals of the forest to clear a path for me? Somehow I'm going to have to bring back that kelp."

"No problem Athena. "

Little did she know, the animals of the forest already had a plan in motion? The beavers, said they would make a raft, heck they were making ten rafts, twenty rafts. Raccoons were making the harnesses for deer to wear to haul the kelp. The sea otters would tow the rafts upriver to the stream, and then the deer would drag it along the side of the stream to the farm. Everyone went into action because they had noticed the changes. Food was scarcer. The stream dried up to almost just a trickle at the end of summer. They saw and felt the effects of the changing climate but didn't know what to do; now they had a mission, to help

SAVE THE PLANET!

Athena just kept trudging along, singing,

"WHERE'S THE OCEAN? WHERE'S THE OCEAN?"

As she rounded the bend of the river, it spread out like a huge fan, in the distance all she could see was water.

WAS THAT THE OCEAN?

It had to be because there were all the animals waiting for her.

Nicki, a deer came up dragging a raft that was piled high with what looked like green fettucine!

"TRY THIS! IT'S KELP!"

Athena took a little nibble, then another, then another and before you knew it she was munching away!

She liked it! Athena liked it!

A roar went up from all the animals gathered around. She liked it!

THERE WAS HOPE FOR THE PLANET.

Athena needed to catch her breath. What a beautiful sight, the ocean and all the animals coming together, to help her save the planet.

With tears in her eyes, she said, “Thank-you, thank-you!

I’M SURE WE JUST SAVED THE PLANET!”

Just then all the birds circled over her with a green cape they’d made of kelp,

because a **SUPERCOW** needs a cape.

When she got back to the farm all the cows had on makeshift gas and burp containers that Mel and the brigades had fashioned from discarded junk. The kelp was sprinkled throughout the pasture. Her calves ate and were so proud of their mother.

"Moo-mmy we love you so much! We're so proud of you for saving the planet!"

"I love you too! It wasn't just me.

IT WAS ALL OF US!

I couldn't have done it without everyone."

WE ALL
SAVED THE PLANET

TOGETHER
8.79

TEACHING MOMENT

Cows, sheep, goats, giraffes, and deer belong to a class of mammals called ruminants. Most ruminants have four stomachs, two-toed feet, and store their food in the first chamber of the stomach, called the rumen. They regurgitate the food from the rumen and chew it again to help further break it down to make it easier to digest. That food is better known as cud. One of the microbes that break down the food produces methane.

Methane, what is methane?

Methane, is created when four hydrogen atoms bond to one atom of carbon, a molecule that's lighter than air. Methane gas, like all other greenhouse gases (which includes water vapor), acts like a blanket around our planet, trapping heat. The right amount and the planets average temperature is a life supporting 59 degrees Fahrenheit. Too little and like Mars, the average temperature is 55 degrees below zero, the South Pole in winter. Too much and like Venus, a comfortable 900 degrees.

Livestock is the largest source of methane gas emissions worldwide, contributing over 28 percent of total emissions. For this reason scientists have stepped up their research.

During lab tests, researchers in Australia found that just 2 percent seaweed in cattle feed could reduce methane emissions by 90 percent. The seaweed apparently inhibits an enzyme that contributes to methane production.

If seaweed proves to be a climate-smart supplement, producing it could be environmentally friendly, too. Growing seaweed doesn't require land, fresh water or fertilizer.